Hello Kitty

Happy Christmas!

HarperCollins *Children's Books*

Christmas is on its way
and Hello Kitty can't wait!

Hello Kitty

Happy Christmas!

© 1976, 2014 SANRIO CO., LTD
First published in the UK by HarperCollins *Children's Books* in 2014
13 5 7 9 10 8 6 4 2
ISBN: 978-0-00-755939-8

Written by Stella Gurney
Designed by Anna Lubecka and Jemma Beal

A CIP catalogue record for this title is available from the British Library. No part of this publication
may be reproduced, stored in a retrieval system or transmitted in any form or by any means,
electronic, mechanical, photocopying, recording or otherwise, without the prior permission of
HarperCollins Publishers Ltd, 77-85 Fulham Palace Road, Hammersmith, London, W6 8JB.

www.harpercollins.co.uk

Printed and bound in China

She is helping Mummy to decorate
the tree. Careful, Hello Kitty!

Guess who has been chosen to be a sparkly star in the school Christmas show? Yes, Hello Kitty!

She practises her dance while Grandma makes her a special costume.

Hello Kitty makes Christmas cards
for all her friends and family.
She uses lots of glitter!

Oops - you've made yourself all
sparkly, too, Hello Kitty!

Hello Kitty has received
lots of Christmas cards, too.
The biggest is from Dear Daniel.

Only a week until Christmas Day!
Daddy takes Hello Kitty shopping.
She wants to spend her pocket
money on Christmas gifts.

She buys a book for Mummy,
a hair bow for Mimmy
and a new tie for Daddy.

Hey, no peeking, Daddy!

Time to wrap the presents
and put them under the tree.

There are lots there already.
Hello Kitty loves trying to
guess what they all are!

Only three days left to Christmas...
Hello Kitty and her family go to
a carol concert on the green.

Everyone joins hands and sings carols around the big tree. Hello Kitty loves a good sing-song!

Ta! Da!

Today it's the Christmas show. All the mummies and daddies have come to see it.

Hello Kitty does her star dance perfectly!
Mummy blows her kisses and Daddy waves.

It's Christmas Eve. Only one day to go!
When Hello Kitty wakes up, everything is
covered in a snowy white blanket.
It's going to be a white Christmas.

Hooray!

Hello Kitty meets her
friends to play in the snow.
Look out, Dear Daniel!

Later, Hello Kitty and Daddy decide to do some baking.

Daddy says Father Christmas
likes gingerbread. Mummy says
she likes gingerbread, too!
Naughty Mummy!

At bedtime Hello Kitty and
Mimmy hang their stockings
by the fireplace.

Don't forget to leave a drink
and snack for Father Christmas
and his reindeers, Hello Kitty.

Hello Kitty is so excited!
She tries to stay awake.

Ho! Ho! Ho!

She wants to say hello
to Father Christmas
when he arrives.
But she falls fast asleep!

It's Christmas morning!

Thump
thump
thum

Did Father
Christmas visit?

Yes he did! Mummy and Daddy
come down in their dressing gowns
and everyone opens their presents.

Time for Christmas dinner!
Grandma and Grandpa have arrived.
Everyone pulls crackers and
puts on their hats.

Bang!

Hello Kitty has had
a wonderful Christmas
She feels very, very lucky.

Happy Christmas, everyone!

The world of

Hello Kitty

Enjoy all of these wonderful Hello Kitty books.

Picture books

Occasion books

Where's Hello Kitty?

Activity books

...and more!

Hello Kitty and friends story book series

...and more!